# HOOPS AND
# HOPES

## BY JAKE MADDOX

text by
Monica Roe

STONE ARCH BOOKS
a capstone imprint

Published by Stone Arch Books, an imprint of Capstone.
1710 Roe Crest Drive
North Mankato, Minnesota 56003
capstonepub.com

Library of Congress Cataloging-in-Publication Data is available on
the Library of Congress website.

ISBN: 9781663911032 (hardcover)
ISBN: 9781663920379 (paperback)
ISBN: 9781663911001 (ebook PDF)

Summary: For twelve-year-old Autumn Holloway, a week at Blazing Hoops wheelchair
basketball camp is a dream come true. She has high hopes that it will be her ticket to
making connections in the adaptive sports community. But Autumn struggles to fit in
with her wealthier roommates. To make matters worse, she has to use a borrowed sports
wheelchair because she doesn't have her own. It takes a chance encounter with the campus
custodial staff to help Autumn realize that no matter where she's from or how she speaks,
she belongs at camp—and on the court—just as much as anyone else.

Image Credits:
Alamy/Tetra Images, cover and throughout; Shutterstock, design elements

Editorial Credits:
Editor: Kristen Mohn; Designer: Bobbie Nuytten; Media Researcher: Jo Miller; Production
Specialist: Katy LaVigne

Thank you to our wheelchair basketball consultant, Jesus Villa.

# TABLE OF CONTENTS

# CHAPTER I

# NOTHING BUT NET

*Swish!*

"Yeah!" Autumn cheered as the basketball swished through the net in front of her house. *Five in a row!*

She leaned forward and spun the smooth push rims of her wheelchair. She hurtled after the ball, determined to catch the rebound. She was a second too late. Instead of landing in her hands, the ball hit her footrest, flew past her outstretched fingers, and bounced away.

Autumn rolled her eyes and chased after the ball. She reached the edge of the driveway and eased her wheelchair off the smooth blacktop and onto the uneven grass. She moved carefully so her wheels wouldn't get stuck and then fished the ball from where it had landed in a flower bed.

The front door opened. "Autumn Grace Holloway, are you tearing up my daisies?"

Autumn laughed. "Not on purpose, Marmee," she called, spinning the ball between her hands. "Just getting in some practice before I leave for camp tomorrow."

Her grandmother grinned back. "Well, leave my flowers out of it!" she said. "Supper's almost ready. And don't be tracking any mess onto my floor!" She glanced at the grass caught in the wheels of Autumn's chair. "I'll get the hose for you."

"I'll be right in," Autumn promised.

Marmee unwound the hose, turned on the spigot, and went inside. Autumn pushed her chair back onto the driveway. She glanced at the door, then at the ball in her lap.

"Just a few more shots," she whispered.

The next morning, she would be headed to Blazing Hoops, a youth wheelchair basketball camp where she'd earned a scholarship. She'd never been away from home for so long before—two whole weeks! She'd never been to a university campus either. Especially one three hours away from Sandy Pines, Georgia, where she and Marmee lived.

The sun was setting. Autumn dribbled a few times beside her wheelchair and narrowed her eyes at the basket. *Thump. Thump. Thump.*

She took aim. *Swishhhhh!* Nothing but net.

"Autumn Grace!" Marmee yelled. "If you're not inside in two minutes, your supper goes to the chickens!"

Autumn wiped her sweaty forehead and grinned. *I'm totally ready*, she thought as she headed to the hose to clean her wheels.

Marmee had made Autumn's favorites for dinner. Baked chicken, mashed potatoes with gravy, and plenty of sides.

"Can't send you off on an empty stomach," she said, loading Autumn's plate with more tomato pie. "Who knows what they'll feed you at camp."

Autumn gulped her milk and grabbed another biscuit. "I better eat up now, then," she said with a laugh. "What time we leaving?"

Marmee picked up the packet from Blazing Hoops. "Registration runs from nine until noon," she said. "We'd best be on the road by seven a.m."

Autumn groaned good-naturedly. "Guess I can manage that," she joked. She'd probably be too excited to sleep anyway.

Marmee sighed. "I can't believe you're leaving me for two weeks," she said. "Going off to a place where you don't know a soul. You nervous?"

Autumn shook her head. "Nope!" she declared. "I can't wait!"

After they cleaned up, Autumn went to finish packing. She organized her things, making sure to include the small toolkit she used for minor wheelchair repairs. She carefully zipped the spending money Marmee had given her into a small purse and tucked it into an inside pocket of her suitcase.

When she was done, Autumn went to tell Marmee good night. Then she brushed her teeth, got into bed, and closed her eyes.

But she was wide awake.

Finally, Autumn gave up on sleep and swung herself back into her wheelchair. She grabbed her hand-me-down tablet off her desk and pulled up the basketball videos she'd saved from last year's Paralympics. She watched the players fly across the court. Spinning, passing, dribbling, moving their wheelchairs in a graceful dance. The ball flew around the court like a meteor. When a chair spun out and skidded onto its side, the players used their powerful arms to push themselves back upright. Sometimes another player reached down to help.

It was amazing. And exactly what Autumn wanted to do. She watched until her eyelids finally grew heavy, then got back into bed.

*Why can't it be morning already?* she thought impatiently.

Blazing Hoops would mean so many firsts for Autumn. For the first time in her life, she was going to get to play basketball. Actual basketball, not just dribbling and shooting baskets in her driveway. A real basketball camp, where she'd learn to play from real college coaches. She'd finally get to play with other people who used wheels like she did. She messed around with her friends at school, of course, playing HORSE and shooting baskets during open gym. But it wasn't quite the same.

She knew other people who had wheelchairs. But they were mostly Marmee's age—or even older. Sandy Pines was a small town, and there were no other kids at Autumn's school who used a wheelchair.

For the first time ever, Autumn was going to fit right in. That was maybe the most exciting thing of all.

# CHAPTER 2

# BLAZING HOOPS

Early the next morning, Marmee loaded Autumn's suitcase and duffel bag into their old sedan. Then Autumn transferred into the passenger seat while Marmee folded up her wheelchair and slid it into the backseat.

As they drove the back roads toward the highway, Autumn wondered if she'd forgotten anything. "You get your medicine refilled?" she asked.

Marmee patted Autumn's knee. "Last Monday." She glanced at Autumn. "You worried about me or you?"

Autumn grinned. "Little of both, I guess. But I'm mostly excited."

Marmee grinned back. "That's my girl!" she said. "You just worry about having the best time of your life. Sandy Pines will be right here waiting for you."

Halfway there, Autumn sniffed the air. "You smell something hot?" she asked.

Marmee was already pulling over. "Dollars to doughnuts, it's that radiator again." She popped the hood and got out.

Even from inside, Autumn could hear the hissing sound the car was making. "Oh, *no*," she groaned.

Marmee was right. The radiator had overheated. They called Autumn's uncle Gary to drive out with some coolant. It was an easy fix, but it was more than an hour until they were back on the road. After that. Marmee had to drive slowly so the car wouldn't overheat again, which lost them even more time.

Autumn flipped stations on the radio and tried not to feel impatient. They couldn't risk tearing up their only car—Marmee needed it to get to work. Still, Autumn glanced at the time. They were going to be late for registration.

*It doesn't matter*, she told herself sternly.

They pulled through the gates of Candler College at twenty minutes after twelve.

"There!" Autumn pointed out the window toward a sign that read: BLAZING HOOPS WHEELCHAIR BASKETBALL CAMP REGISTRATION INSIDE.

"Thank goodness this old thing made it," Marmee joked, patting the dashboard. She drove past big, leafy trees; beautiful stone buildings; and a few parking lots full of shiny, new cars.

Finally, they reached the registration building. Marmee pulled up in front and unloaded Autumn's wheelchair. Autumn slid from the passenger seat into her chair and rolled toward the entrance. Not wanting to be another minute late, she pressed the button to open the door and went in. *Marmee will catch up,* she thought and hurried inside.

Inside, the building was glossy and fancy-looking, with high ceilings and lots of wood and glass everywhere.

*Like something straight out of a movie*, Autumn thought, taking it all in.

Long tables were set up along the back of the room, with "Welcome Campers!" signs taped to them. But there was nobody in the room. Then a young man wearing workout clothes came through a side door.

"Can I help you?" he asked. "I'm Carlos." He reached out and shook Autumn's hand.

"I'm here for Blazing Hoops," Autumn said. "Sorry, I know I'm a little late."

Carlos nodded. "You must be Autumn Holloway," he said. "We thought maybe you weren't coming."

His smile and voice were friendly, but Autumn still flushed. "We got held up on the way." *Why can't our car be reliable when it matters?*

"Not a problem," Carlos assured her. "We'll get you settled in."

Marmee came in carrying Autumn's duffel bag and suitcase. "I'm Margaret Holloway," she said, reaching to shake Carlos's hand. "Autumn's grandmomma."

"Nice to meet you," Carlos said politely. "Let's get Autumn signed in and over to her dorm. The other girls will be headed to lunch, but we'll get her caught up."

He handed Marmee some forms to fill out and then gave them directions to a building called Richardson Hall. The dormitory would be "home" for the next two weeks.

"Someone will meet you there soon," Carlos said.

"Should I stay until she's settled in?" Marmee asked quickly. Autumn could tell that Marmee was more nervous than Autumn was.

"I'll be okay," Autumn assured her, thinking of the long drive home. She didn't want Marmee driving after dark in case the car acted up again. "Once we get my stuff dropped off, you can head out."

Richardson Hall was made of rough, gray stone and looked a bit like a tiny castle, except for the automatic door at one side. They found Autumn's room on the first floor. Autumn punched in the combination she'd been given to open the door.

Inside was a common living room and kitchenette, a double bedroom off to each side, and a large, accessible bathroom. Three of the four beds had people's things on them. Marmee put Autumn's luggage on the one empty bed.

Autumn felt like she was missing out already. It looked like everyone else had arrived hours ago.

*Hope it's not too late to make friends*, Autumn thought. She tried to brush the sudden, insecure thought away.

"Want to unpack?" Marmee asked.

"No time," came a crisp voice from behind them.

Autumn spun her chair. A woman wearing black sweats and a whistle was in the doorway.

Her wheelchair was beautiful—sleek, black, and streamlined.

"I'm Tara," she said. "One of the coaches and counselors." She smiled at Autumn. "There'll be plenty of time to unpack later. Let's grab you some lunch and get to the gym. First practice session starts soon."

Suddenly, Autumn was hugging Marmee goodbye and waving as her grandmother drove away. The churning in Autumn's stomach felt like excitement and fear mixed together.

Tara pulled up beside Autumn. "Did you drop your sports wheelchair at the gym already?"

Autumn froze. "I . . . don't have a sports chair."

# CHAPTER 3

# ROOMMATES

Tara frowned. "You didn't get the packing list?" Her tone wasn't unkind, but the question flooded Autumn with discomfort. "It was e-mailed to all the campers."

Autumn rolled her chair back and forth. Sandy Pines didn't have good Wi-Fi coverage. Autumn only got online once or twice a week when Marmee drove her to the library, and she hadn't been able to read the packing list until a few days ago. By the time Autumn had discovered that campers were supposed to bring a sports chair, it had been too late to do anything about it. She'd slipped that page out of the information she'd printed before giving it to Marmee.

Besides, even if she'd told Marmee, where would they borrow a sports chair last-minute? Just getting to the city for Autumn's yearly wheelchair check took an hour each way.

Autumn had decided there was no point in worrying Marmee with something she couldn't do anything about.

Now, Autumn gathered her courage and forced herself to look Tara in the eye. "Are there any loaner chairs here?"

Tara's forehead furrowed in thought. "A few," she said. "But I think they've all been lent out already." Then she smiled. "No worries. Let's get your lunch, and we'll figure something out, okay?"

"Thanks," Autumn replied. She was hungry and eager to meet everyone at last.

Tara led Autumn across a smooth, paved path that crossed campus to the dining hall. She got Autumn a carry-out lunch from a smiling woman behind a counter, and then they rolled over to the big athletic center.

As they went through the automatic doors, Autumn's heart beat faster. Finally, she was here!

"The girls are already practicing," Tara said as they headed to the basketball courts.

Autumn tried to look everywhere at once, from the shiny fitness equipment to the huge swimming pool to the indoor track. But the steady *thunk-thunking* from the bouncing balls and the squeak of the wheels on the court was what really thrilled her.

Carlos met them at the door to the courts. "Where's your gym chair, Autumn?" he asked cheerfully, glancing at his clipboard.

"Bit of a mix-up," Tara said smoothly. "Do we still have anything in the loaner closet?"

Carlos tapped his chin. "I think there might be one left," he said. "But it's missing a couple parts. I can take it over to maintenance later and see what they can do."

"That's great," Autumn said quickly. "I'll just use my regular chair until then."

Behind Carlos, she glimpsed a blur of wheels and bodies zipping all over the court. She tapped her fingers on her rims, eager to get in there and play.

But Carlos shook his head. "Sorry, Autumn. I can't let you on the court on those wheels."

Autumn bit back a protest. "Is something wrong with my chair?" she asked. Back home, she always played ball in her regular chair.

Carlos smiled. "Nothing at all. But it's not built for the court." He stepped out of the doorway and pointed at the players. "See what I mean?"

Autumn stared in amazement at the speed and agility of the girls warming up on the basketball court. Their chairs were custom fitted with low-profile backrests, tucked away footrests, and extra caster wheels in the rear to keep them from falling backward. The wheels were slanted, allowing for tight turns and swift maneuvering.

Autumn sighed. She'd seen chairs like this, just never in person. But she'd looked them up online at the library enough times to know how much they cost—way too much.

"Hey, don't worry!" Carlos said. "Tara, how about you take over practice while I find that chair and get it to maintenance right away?"

Tara nodded. Then she rolled onto the court and blew her whistle.

"We'll get you on the court by tomorrow, Autumn," Carlos added. "Promise."

Autumn rolled to the sidelines, mesmerized by the action. About twenty girls, all close to her age, zipped around the court in sports chairs. They weaved and darted, blocking for each other, using incredible ball-handling skills, and effortlessly taking shots.

Tara and the other counselor-coaches led the girls through some drills. They practiced ball handling under pressure, passing, and shooting while being guarded.

"Remember!" Tara shouted. "You can only wheel twice without dribbling or it's a traveling violation!"

Autumn's excitement bubbled. She rolled back and forth in place, impatiently. *I can't wait to get out there!*

Practice finished, and her chair still wasn't ready. The girls broke into groups and headed to the dorms to relax until dinner. Autumn followed them and met the other three who shared her dorm suite— Coral Ramos, Bree Harrington, and Ashti Singh.

Coral lived in Atlanta, and her moms were both engineers. Bree's father was a heart surgeon in Charlotte, North Carolina. Ashti's parents were professors at Candler College.

"Can you believe the food at lunch today?" Bree said as they all hung out in the living room. Everyone except Autumn had showered and changed. Bree wrinkled her nose. "It was like leftover leftovers!"

Ashti and Coral giggled.

Autumn didn't say anything. Her carry-out lunch from the dining hall had seemed fine.

Bree continued, "Let's order in pizza tonight— then we won't have to abuse our stomachs before practice tomorrow."

"Great idea!" Ashti grabbed her phone. "My family always orders from Perfect Pi. Everyone in?"

Coral nodded eagerly. "Greek style is my favorite."

Autumn thought about the spending money Marmee had given her the previous night. It had to last her two weeks.

"I'll stick to the dining hall tonight," she finally said. "But thanks anyway."

\* \* \*

Autumn headed to the dining hall alone, telling herself she didn't really mind not getting pizza. The ride across campus was beautiful. The afternoon sun shone like fire on the stone buildings, and the paths were smooth beneath her wheels.

As she zipped across a grassy, tree-lined clearing, Autumn watched a group of college students playing Frisbee on the lawn. Watching them dive for the Frisbee made her eager to get onto the court tomorrow.

Inside the dining hall, Autumn wheeled into line. She smiled at the cashier who scanned her meal card. "Thank you, ma'am," she said. "Have a great evening."

The woman smiled back. "You too, hon." Her name tag said Keoko.

Autumn balanced the tray on her lap and looked for a place at a table. She finally spotted an empty space at one of them, and a girl with a long, black ponytail adjusted her wheelchair to make room. "Hi," she said cheerfully. "I'm Amira."

"Hi. I'm Autumn." Autumn put her tray on the table and pulled up beside Amira. She looked around the table, crowded with laughing, chatting girls.

"Wow," Autumn said quietly. "This is a first."

"You mean not having the only set of wheels in the room?" Amira grinned. "Nice, huh?"

Autumn grinned back. "It sure is!"

# CHAPTER 4

# NEW WHEELS

The next morning, Autumn and her roommates went to breakfast together before practice.

"It's still gross," Bree muttered, looking at the food selections.

Autumn, who was in front of Bree, cringed. She glanced around, hoping none of the staff had heard Bree's complaints. Didn't she care about their feelings?

"I like it," Autumn said.

Bree shrugged. "Guess we all *like* different things," she said in a slightly twangy voice.

Autumn frowned. Was she imagining it, or had Bree just imitated the way she talked?

She thought about how Bree had raised her eyebrows last night when Autumn told them that her grandmother worked as the receptionist for a pest-control company.

"That's . . . nice," Bree had said.

Rolling up to the counter, Ashti grabbed some fruit and yogurt. "It's not so bad," she said. "My parents and I eat here a lot during the school year."

When she got to the cashier, Autumn grinned. "Hi, Keoko!" she said, recognizing a familiar face. "Nice to see you again." It really was, Autumn realized as Keoko smiled back. Autumn almost felt relieved to see her. She glanced around the cafeteria, hoping to see Amira but didn't.

The girls finished quickly and headed to practice. In the gym, Carlos and Tara were already warmed up.

"Autumn!" Carlos called. "Come on, I've got your wheels!"

Her heart pounding, Autumn followed Carlos over to a blue sports wheelchair.

"It's not perfect," Carlos cautioned as Autumn locked the brakes on her own chair and got ready to swing herself over. "But the maintenance folks said it should hold up fine."

"It looks great!" Autumn exclaimed.

She could hardly keep the chair still as Carlos helped her tighten the safety belts low on her hips and ankles. The chair was more streamlined than hers, and Autumn couldn't wait to let it loose on the court.

"Always keep the belts on when you're on the court, so you won't go flying when you take a tumble," Carlos said.

His warning made Autumn even more excited. Back home, her teachers were always telling her *not* to take chances. But here at Blazing Hoops, they seemed to expect that she would. Just like any other athlete.

Tara rolled into the gym and blew her whistle. "Circle up!" she called.

The girls moved their wheelchairs into a large circle, and Tara and Carlos led them through some passing drills. Autumn was thrilled as she bounced and caught the ball with the others. She discovered that her passing skills were as good as most of the other girls'.

Tara moved around the circle, offering pointers. "You can lean over a little farther," she suggested after watching Autumn pass a few times. "These sports chairs have a much wider base of support than everyday ones."

Autumn followed her instructions and was rewarded with an extra-hard pass to Ashti.

"Good one, Autumn!" Ashti said, catching it.

Next, they broke into groups to practice shooting drills. Autumn and Bree were in the same group. Autumn had to admit Bree was a good player. Her sports chair was a sleek, shiny green, and she was incredibly fast.

Tara blew her whistle. "First drill, Twenty-One Up! Line up at the free-throw line, ladies!"

"Heads-up, cowgirl!" Bree called, throwing a hard pass at Autumn.

Autumn quickly snagged the ball and launched it toward the net.

*Swish!*

* * *

There was a letter in the mail holder when the girls got back to their room. Bree pulled it out.

"It's for Autumn," she said, flipping it over. "Who's Marmee? That's a funny name."

"My grandmomma," Autumn replied.

Bree snorted. "'Grandmomma'?" she echoed. This time there was no mistaking the intentional twanginess in her voice.

Coral giggled. Ashti looked down at the floor.

Autumn bristled. "Yeah," she said, grabbing the letter. "And her name isn't funny." She rolled to her room, suddenly wanting to be alone.

A minute later, Ashti knocked. "Can I come in?"

Autumn took a deep breath. "Of course." It was Ashti's room too, after all.

"Don't mind Bree," Ashti said. "She clearly doesn't know that 'Marmee' is from *Little Women*. Pretty cool nickname," she added.

Autumn tried to smile. "Thanks."

But secretly, she wondered if she could trust any of these girls—even Ashti.

*Maybe*, Autumn thought sadly, *I'm just too different to fit in here.*

# CHAPTER 5

# MISS FIX-IT

*Thunk! Thunk!* The ball slapped hard against Autumn's palm as she dribbled. Her borrowed blue sports chair shot up the court like a rocket.

"Autumn!" Amira yelled from inside their team's baseline. "I'm open!"

It was the next afternoon, and Autumn felt a little better about things. Reading Marmee's letter had helped. Thoughtful as ever, Marmee had mailed it two days before camp started so Autumn would have it right away.

*I'm so proud of you,* the letter had said. *And this is just the first step, I promise. We're going to find a way to get you into this world.*

Marmee's faith in her made Autumn determined to stop worrying about the small stuff. Who cared if she didn't fit in with her roommates? It wouldn't stop her. She had to focus on what really mattered. Getting the scholarship to Blazing Hoops had been the opportunity of a lifetime. Now it was up to her to make something of it—to figure out how to get more seriously involved in wheelchair ball.

Suddenly, Autumn saw a flash of bright green on her left. Bree was closing in.

*I don't think so,* Autumn thought to herself.

She and Bree had been butting heads all morning. Battling fiercely for the ball after almost every tip-off. Cutting each other off, wheels clipping dangerously close to each other.

Now, Autumn poured on the speed and battled her way up the court. The scrimmage was almost over—less than a minute on the clock—and her team was down by two points. Autumn's shoulder and arm muscles burned as her gloved hands skillfully moved the ball and her wheelchair close enough to pass to Amira.

*Crash!* Autumn's chair jolted as the front of Bree's chair clipped her from the side.

"Hey!" Autumn yelled. She darted a glance at the sidelines, but Carlos hadn't seen Bree sideswipe her. If he had, he would have definitely called the foul.

Bree smiled slyly. "Sorry," she said. Her eyes were bright blue against her sweaty skin. And they didn't look sorry.

Autumn gritted her teeth and ignored Bree. She zeroed in on Amira, still waiting below the basket. Lightning-fast, Autumn cut a path through the tangle of players. She bounced the ball once, twice, then spun her chair to a halt.

She launched the ball into the air just as Bree lunged to block her.

Autumn smiled in satisfaction as the ball flew just beyond Bree's outstretched fingers. It sailed through the air, straight to Amira, who caught it and launched a perfect shot.

*Bzzzzzz!* The buzzer sounded as the clock ran out.

A split second later, the ball swished through the net. The girls on Autumn's team erupted in cheers.

Carlos blew his whistle. "Great job, girls," he said. "Let's call it a day. The gym will be open from seven to nine this evening for anyone who wants extra practice."

"Great pass," Amira told Autumn as they headed to the locker rooms.

"Thanks," Autumn answered, feeling proud. "Piece of cake. And nice basket!" she added.

She ignored the dirty look Bree gave her.

After they changed, Autumn headed to the dorm with her roommates.

"Darn!" Coral said when they were halfway across campus. "My footrest is loose." She leaned over and peered at the footplate of her silver sports chair.

The girls all looked over. Autumn saw the problem. "Looks like a screw's about to fall out."

Coral groaned. "Probably loosened up when I wiped out before halftime."

Autumn thought it looked like an easy fix. And she had plenty of spare hardware in her toolkit.

"You want help with that when we get back to the dorm?" Autumn asked.

Coral looked surprised. "We usually take my chair to my seating guy for repairs," she said. "His office is just ten minutes from our house."

Ashti nodded. "Oh, yeah. We practically have my ATP on speed dial, especially during playing season. Her office is pretty close to campus," she added, looking at Coral. "You want her number?"

Autumn thought about the hour-long drive to visit her own assistive technology professional. She saw her ATP every year for a wheelchair checkup and adjustments. She and Marmee could handle most minor repairs on their own—Autumn had loved helping her uncle Gary take apart and fix stuff on his farm since she was little.

"Seriously," Autumn told Coral, "this is an easy fix." She was surprised at how little her roommates seemed to know about maintaining their own equipment. Maybe it was because they were used to just dropping it off to be repaired?

Coral looked doubtful. But back in the dorm, she swung out of her chair and onto the common-room sofa. Autumn went to get her toolkit.

Rejoining the other girls, Autumn locked her brakes and tossed her toolkit to the floor. Then she carefully slid herself down the front of her wheelchair and onto the floor beside Coral's now-empty sports chair. Ashti put on a movie, while Bree went to take a shower.

Autumn tilted Coral's wheelchair onto its side to work on the footplate. As she pulled tools from her kit and started to work, Autumn felt a surge of calm fill her. She always felt at home when she did anything mechanical.

She worked steadily, unscrewing the footplate and pulling it free. The screw was stripped, so she rummaged in her repair kit for a matching screw and easily re-attached it. When she was done, she flipped the chair upright again. Still sitting on the floor, Autumn gave the footplate an experimental tug to make sure it was nice and tight.

"Wow!" Coral glanced up from the movie and grinned. "That's amazing, Autumn. Thank you!"

"Can you show me how to do that?" Ashti asked. "I never thought about learning to do repairs myself," she admitted. "But you're a regular Miss Fix-It!"

Autumn blushed. *All three of them can probably just buy brand-new chairs instead of making repairs*, she thought. She brushed the thought away. Feeling jealous wouldn't solve anything.

Bree wheeled out of the bathroom, toweling off her blond hair. She was wearing a purple hoodie with the Blazing Hoops logo on the front.

"Nice shirt," Coral said. "Where'd you get it?"

"Campus store," Bree replied. "I'm going back tomorrow for a few more things."

Autumn had to admit Bree's hoodie was nice. She wondered how much it cost, but she was pretty sure she knew the answer: *way more than I have.*

# CHAPTER 6

# NOT ONE OF THEM

As the days passed, Autumn pushed herself harder than ever. The girls had both morning and afternoon practices each day, with optional extra playing time in the evenings.

"I'm open!" she shouted, hands poised to catch. It was almost eight p.m., and just a small group of girls had stayed for the late session.

Autumn never missed a chance to play. She was determined to take advantage of every minute of court time. Who knew when she'd get another chance?

Plus, the scholarship she'd been awarded to attend Blazing Hoops this summer was for a first-time experience only. She wouldn't be able to afford full price to come again next year. She was going to have to earn a way to return—somehow. Because now that she'd gotten a taste of what it was really like to play ball, she never wanted it to end.

A girl named Laquiana, playing forward, flew up the court, ponytail whipping and wheels a blur. She was strong and fast, and Autumn was glad they were playing on the same side tonight. Laquiana spun her chair, stopped, and flung the ball in a perfect arc toward Autumn.

But Bree snatched it from the air a second before Autumn could reach it.

*Argh!* How could she have missed Bree behind her?

Autumn raced after Bree, but it was too late. Bree darted through a tiny gap in the crowded court, leaving Autumn to battle through a web of defensive players.

Bree reached the key and took the shot. It bounced off the rim, but Amira, who was playing on her side today, rebounded it.

*Swish!*

"Yes!" Amira cheered. The girls on her team whooped in triumph.

Autumn blew out a hard breath. *It's just practice,* she reminded herself. They weren't even starting real games until the second week. The big game would be the final night of camp.

When practice let out, Autumn wiped her sweaty face on a towel and gulped down a bottle of water.

"You coming back to the dorm, Autumn?" Ashti called from the gym doorway.

"I'll catch up!" Autumn called back. She gathered her stuff from the sidelines while the other girls trickled out. She noticed a few stray balls on the court and started to collect them in the metal rack.

"Thanks, Autumn." Tara brought the last ball over to the rack. "This isn't the first time you've picked up after practice," she added. "Carlos and I appreciate it. It shows character," Tara said.

Tara gathered up her gym bag, and she and Autumn rolled to the doors. Autumn waited while Tara turned off the lights and locked up. Then they headed outside together. It was growing dark, and the campus was softly lit by street lamps along the narrow paths.

"You've got talent, Autumn," Tara said as they cruised along the paved paths toward the dorms. "Did you ever play back home?"

Autumn shook her head. "Not too many wheelchair ball teams out where I live," she said. "Actually none. I'm the only one on wheels in my whole school."

She almost told Tara how Marmee used to bring a rolling desk chair to the driveway so she and Autumn could play together. But she stopped herself. Autumn got the impression the other girls—Bree, at least— thought where she lived sounded strange. What if

Tara thought so too? But Tara nodded knowingly.

"That's too bad," she said. "I really wish there were more teams out there. You're from a small town?"

Autumn laughed. "Not even!" She told Tara about Sandy Pines and the little house she and Marmee lived in down a long, dirt road. "We only go into the nearest big city a few times a year," she added. "I love where I live, but there are a couple things I wouldn't mind having a little closer."

Tara didn't laugh. "I get it," she said. "I grew up in a small town too. Maybe a little bigger than Sandy Pines," she added with a smile, "but not much."

"How did you get into basketball, then?" Autumn asked eagerly.

"After high school, I came here for college," Tara explained. "I found the wheelchair basketball team pretty much by accident. And I just never left!"

"That's great," Autumn said, but Tara's words made her feel glum. Even if she and Marmee found a way to pay for it, it would be years before she was old enough for college. She'd practically be ancient by then.

They were halfway along the path that cut through the grassy area in the middle of campus. Tara suddenly stopped, shoved her hands backward on her rims, and flipped her chair into a perfect wheelie.

Not do be outdone, Autumn did one too. Wheelies were easy once you found your balance point.

"Nice one," Tara told Autumn after they'd both held the wheelie for more than a minute. "You really do have natural talent," she said again, gracefully setting her front wheels back onto the path. "You should think about getting a sports chair of your own—a good one."

Autumn thought about her borrowed blue chair. It rattled a little when she really got going during practice. But it still felt amazing to her—like going from a pony to a Thoroughbred.

"I'd love one," she finally said. "But our insurance doesn't cover it."

Autumn's health insurance covered her regular wheelchair, which was great for everyday stuff. But sports chairs weren't considered "medical necessities."

Tara sighed. "I know. But there are some other options. There are grant programs that help cover the cost of equipment for adaptive sports. Or even crowdfunding, church fundraisers, stuff like that."

Autumn stiffened. It wasn't that those ideas weren't good ones. But she and Marmee took care of things themselves. They always had.

She sighed, thinking about her roommates. Bree and Coral and Ashti probably never had to ask strangers for money to get their basketball chairs. It didn't seem fair.

As if she could read Autumn's thoughts, Tara asked, "How're you getting on with the other girls? Making friends?"

Autumn shrugged. "I guess. Ashti's nice."

Ashti had actually been friendly from the

start. She hadn't laughed about Marmee's name or Autumn's accent like Bree and Coral had.

But Autumn knew she still wasn't one of them.

It didn't make sense. For the first time in her life, Autumn was surrounded by other girls who used wheels and loved basketball, just like her.

But somehow those things weren't enough to make her feel like she fit in.

# CHAPTER 7

# BENCHED!

Two days later, flyers started appearing around campus. Camp was already halfway over, and different end-of-camp committees were looking for volunteers. There was a decorations committee, a prize committee, and others. Everything would be presented at the banquet after the final basketball game.

As she rolled past the library on her way to the mail room with a postcard for Marmee, Autumn paused to read a flyer for the staff appreciation committee. That sounded like fun—everyone who worked for the camp had been great. Carlos and Tara, Keoko and the dining hall staff, the workers who cleaned the gym each morning. Autumn was even on a first-name basis with Edna and Sergei, two housekeeping employees who kept the dorm halls and shared spaces clean. It would be nice to help think of a way to say thanks.

*If I have the time*, Autumn reminded herself. She was here to play ball, not hang decorations or choose prizes.

She got to practice just in time to hear Carlos call out the positions for the morning scrimmage.

"Harrington and Holloway!" he shouted. "Center circle! On the double!"

Autumn stifled a groan at hearing Bree's last name and hers called together for tip-off. Of course.

She clenched her jaw and rolled to the center circle. Bree quickly followed, and the rest of the players took their positions on the court behind the two girls.

Carlos blew his whistle and tossed the ball. Autumn and Bree both lunged for it.

Autumn got there a second sooner. She slapped the

ball away from Bree and dribbled up the court.

*Take that!* she thought with satisfaction.

Her good mood didn't last long. In the second quarter, she and Bree both went for a rebound and collided. Autumn yelped as pain shot through her wrist.

*Tweet!* Carlos blew his whistle and ran over. "You girls okay?" he asked.

Autumn glared at Bree. "I was until she bulldozed me," she grumbled, rubbing her throbbing wrist.

Bree, who was cradling her own hand, glared too. "Like you wouldn't have run me over if you could've," she shot back.

Tara raced over. "That's already starting to swell," she said, frowning at Bree's jammed finger. "And you're going to have a nasty bruise," she added, nodding at Autumn's wrist. "Let's get you two checked out."

In the health center, the athletic trainer examined them. She wrapped them up and gave both girls the same instructions. "Keep ice on it for forty-eight hours and leave the wrap on except for showers. You'll probably be able to get back on the court after that."

"Forty-eight hours?" Autumn cried. "The final game is five days away! I can't be out for two whole days!"

The trainer shrugged. "Sorry," she said. "Afraid you're both benched for a bit."

Autumn couldn't believe it. Two entire days off the court? It was impossible!

But Tara was firm. "It's not the end of the world," she told them as the girls waited for the lift van to take them to the dorm. "Better safe than sorry."

"This stinks," Bree muttered, glaring at Autumn.

Autumn glared back. "At least we agree on something."

\* \* \*

Autumn spent the afternoon in her room, icing her wrist and watching wheelchair basketball on Ashti's computer, which she had said Autumn could use. If she couldn't go to afternoon practice, at least she could work on her strategy.

But close to dinnertime, Autumn couldn't take it anymore. She had to get some fresh air.

Autumn rolled carefully into the suite's common area and bit back a groan. Coral and Ashti were still at afternoon practice, but Bree had transferred herself onto the sofa. She was watching a show on her tablet while she iced her hand.

The two girls ignored each other. Using mostly her good arm and switching from rim to rim now and then, Autumn slowly rolled out to the front lobby of the building. She looked at the bulletin board until she found the flyer she was searching for.

Autumn copied down the information. Then she rubbed her still-swollen wrist, thinking. She had two entire days to fill, so she had no excuse. She was going to join the staff appreciation committee.

Autumn sighed. "Not exactly how I'd planned to spend my time," she muttered to the empty lobby.

Back in the suite, the common room was now empty. But from inside Bree and Coral's bedroom, Autumn could hear Bree talking on the phone. She sounded upset.

Autumn paused. Bree sounded close to tears, even through the door. She thought about checking on her. But then she remembered all the times she and Bree had clashed this week, like when Bree had made fun of her accent or cut her off on the court. If it weren't for their stupid collision this morning, Autumn wouldn't be stuck with a sore wrist and two days on the bench.

*Bree doesn't need my help*, Autumn decided. *She'd probably bite my head off if I tried, anyway.*

Decision made, Autumn rolled into her own bedroom and shut the door. Marmee would probably be disappointed in her if she knew.

Then again, Marmee hadn't raised a doormat, either.

# CHAPTER 8

# JUST THIS ONCE

The staff appreciation committee met later in the afternoon in the downstairs lounge. Amira was there, along with some other girls Autumn hadn't talked to much. There was music and snacks, and they spent the first hour just hanging out and snacking.

Autumn learned she wasn't the only one whose family wasn't wealthy. There were girls at Blazing Hoops from all over. There was Consuela, whose parents were both paramedics, and Emma, whose single mother worked in a flower shop.

Autumn let herself relax a little. Maybe she hadn't given things enough of a chance.

The girls had fun, but they didn't get too much staff appreciation planning done. Soon it was getting to be evening, and everyone headed off to dinner.

Autumn decided not to strain her wrist by pushing herself all the way to the dining hall. Tara had dropped off some boxed meals for her and Bree earlier. That would be good enough.

When Autumn got back to the suite, Ashti and Coral were watching a show in the common room.

"Hey, Autumn," Ashti said with a smile. "We're having movie night. You can help pick."

Coral chimed in. "We're getting takeout too. Do you like Thai?"

Autumn was about to reply that she'd never tried Thai food and would pass. But suddenly, she stopped. Ashti and Coral were inviting her to enjoy dinner and a movie. She'd just had a good time with the other girls at the meeting.

*Why shouldn't I accept?* Autumn wondered. *Just this once?*

"Sure," she answered. "I like pretty much anything."

When the food arrived, Autumn quickly realized her mistake. None of the few restaurants in Sandy Pines cost much—you could easily get a whole dinner for less than ten dollars. So she nearly gasped when she saw the takeout bill. The spending money Marmee had given her would just cover the cost. She definitely wouldn't be able to afford any Blazing Hoops gear now—not even a water bottle.

Autumn went to her room and got the money for her share.

"Here you go!" Ashti said as she handed Autumn a plate filled with food. "Their pad thai is the best in town—my parents and I probably order it twice a month."

Autumn balanced the plate on her lap and tried to enjoy the movie and the Thai food. Beside her, Ashti and Coral were sampling food from the takeout boxes, gushing over their favorites.

"Oops!" Coral accidentally dripped some sauce on her Blazing Hoops hoodie. "That's totally going to leave a stain!" She dabbed a napkin over the spot. "Maybe I'll head to the bookstore and grab a new one tomorrow."

Autumn couldn't believe what she was hearing. It was another reminder: *I'm not like these girls. Money doesn't grow on trees for me.*

She wouldn't forget again.

A few minutes later, Bree came out of her bedroom, balancing her towel and shower stuff on her lap. Her eyes looked red.

"Everything okay?" Coral asked quietly.

"Fine," Bree said quickly.

"How's your finger?" Autumn asked before she could stop herself.

Bree shrugged. "I'll live. Sorry to disappoint." She disappeared into the bathroom before Autumn could reply.

Autumn and Bree were finally cleared to play again.

"But take it easy," Tara said, looking straight at Autumn. "This is supposed to be fun."

Autumn, already headed to the court, barely heard her. She had lost time to make up for.

For the next several days, Autumn pushed herself extra hard in practice, determined to be ready for the final game. Tara had reminded them it was only an exhibition game, but Autumn wasn't about to go into it unprepared. Most of the girls had a chance to play year-round, but this might be the only time Autumn ever got to play in a game, and she wanted to make Marmee proud.

At least she and Bree had stopped tangling on the court since their collision. They still didn't talk more than necessary, but they left each other alone—mostly.

After practice, Autumn, Emma, and Amira hurried off to the third staff appreciation committee meeting.

The final game and banquet were coming up fast, and they needed to get things settled.

Junta, a third-year camper and committee head, called the meeting to order.

"Okay! We're in pretty good shape overall, and we've stayed within the budget that the donors gave us. We've got gifts and cards for Carlos and Tara, the athletic director, and the counselors. Besides getting the gifts wrapped and cards signed, I think we just need to decide who'll present them at the banquet."

Autumn suddenly thought of something. "But we haven't decided what to get for the housekeeping and dining hall staff," she pointed out. "Or maintenance."

There was a pause. Some girls looked surprised or confused. But Autumn noticed that Emma nodded in agreement.

Junta blinked. "That's thoughtful," she said slowly. "But the other times I've been to camp, we've sort of stuck to honoring the people who've made camp great for us."

Autumn frowned. "But those workers do that too! They clean our dorms and keep us fed. And someone in maintenance fixed the sports chair I've been using."

Another girl chimed in. "True. That's their job all year, though—not just during camp."

Emma spoke up. "Does that matter?" she asked softly. "Keoko has been making special meals for me because of my allergies. They're really going out of their way for us."

"That's sweet," Junta said. "But the committee really only focuses on everyone who's helped us with basketball. How would we even know what sort of gift the maintenance staff would like?"

They took a vote. Emma, Amira, and Consuela voted for Autumn's suggestion. Junta and five others voted against it. *So much for that,* Autumn thought.

# CHAPTER 9

# SHINY ON THE OUTSIDE

Autumn was full of frustration. After the meeting, she went for a long ride around campus to clear her head. She shoved hard on her push rims, glad her wrist was better. She rolled fast over the paved paths, crisscrossing campus without paying attention to direction. When she finally stopped to rest her tired shoulders, she didn't recognize where she was.

*Whoops.* Autumn studied the unfamiliar stone buildings—*all* the buildings seemed to be stone, so it was hard to tell them apart. She tried to figure out which side of the big campus she was on. She followed one path for a while, and then another, but nothing looked familiar.

Then her chair made a scraping noise. Autumn leaned over to inspect it and groaned. *Great.* One of the casters at the front of the chair was sticking, making the chair move unevenly. Maybe she'd gotten some debris or a small rock caught in it while rolling over one of the cobblestone paths.

Autumn sighed. If only she'd brought her toolkit with her.

"Hi, Autumn!" someone called.

Autumn turned and smiled. It was Keoko, from the dining hall. "Keoko! Hey, nice haircut!"

Keoko smiled back. "Thanks! What brings you to this side of campus?"

Autumn explained how she'd gone for a ride and gotten lost. "To top things off, I banged up my wheels too!" She showed Keoko the damaged caster.

Keoko took a look and said, "Come with me."

Autumn followed her to the back entrance of a building, past a small sign that said FACILITIES. Keoko led her inside and called, "Nathaniel! We need your magic touch!"

"Coming!" A young man came in from a side door, wiping his hands on a rag. "What can I do for you?"

Keoko introduced Autumn and explained about the broken caster.

"No problem." Nathaniel crouched down to inspect it. "I worked on this chair last week."

"So, you're one who fixed it for me!" Autumn said. "It's worked really well. Thanks for tuning it up. And I'm sorry—I know I should have left it in the gym and switched to my other chair. But I was late to a meeting."

Nathaniel just shrugged. "No worries." He and Keoko led Autumn to a small break room full of comfortable chairs. Autumn transferred into an armchair so Nathaniel could take her chair to the maintenance shop.

"Want a snack?" Keoko offered Autumn a cookie from a tin. Several other employees taking their afternoon breaks joined them. They munched their cookies and chatted quietly.

Autumn finished a cookie and was surprised to find herself completely relaxed. She looked around and realized why. Everyone in the break room reminded her of people in Sandy Pines. They had uniform shirts embroidered with their names and tools in their belts. They were working-class, like Marmee.

Like her.

Autumn sighed deeply. It felt good to be here. But it also felt good to be out on the court, weaving and darting toward the basket. Feeling the slap of the ball in her palm and the rush of adrenaline when she made a perfect basket.

But could she have both? Could she belong in both worlds?

Keoko heard her sigh. "Heavy thoughts?" she asked.

Before she knew it, Autumn had told Keoko everything. How she'd expected so much from Blazing Hoops and felt so much pressure to make the most of it. How she'd been so excited to meet other girls who used wheels but hadn't expected to feel so out of place.

"It doesn't make any sense!" Autumn finally burst out.

But Keoko smiled knowingly. Nathaniel, who'd come back with her repaired chair, nodded. "Makes a lot of sense, actually," he said.

Autumn blinked. "It does?"

Keoko shrugged. "We know how you feel. We work here all year."

Autumn saw what they meant. Working service jobs at an expensive college must be hard too.

"Do people make fun of you?" she asked, remembering how Bree had imitated her accent on the first day.

Nathaniel laughed. "Not openly. Sure, some professors—and students—act like we're beneath them. Or invisible. But some are plenty nice. And any who underestimate me—well, that's their problem, not mine."

Autumn remembered how friendly Ashti always was, and she came from a well-off family. Not everyone with money acted high and mighty all the time.

"Money doesn't fix everything," Keoko added, as if reading Autumn's mind. "Everyone's carrying some sort of load—no matter how shiny things look on the outside."

Autumn thought about how upset Bree had sounded on the phone the other day and how red-eyed she'd been when she came out of her bedroom.

*Did I give up on making friends too quickly? Is there still time to try and fix that?*

After thanking Nathaniel and Keoko and getting directions, Autumn headed back across campus. When she reached the grassy middle area that Keoko had called the *quad,* she saw Bree parked under a big, shady tree. She was doing something on her phone.

Autumn started to roll past. Then she stopped.

"Looks like your finger's feeling better," she said, watching Bree scroll rapidly through her phone.

Bree half-looked up. "Yeah," she said coolly.

Autumn took a breath. Bree wasn't going to make this easy. But enough was enough.

"Look," Autumn said, "I'm glad we've stopped messing with each other on the court. So why can't we just get along? What'd I ever do to you?"

Bree bristled. "What do you mean?"

"Come on," Autumn persisted. "You started in on me the second day. Remember making fun of my accent?"

Bree blushed. "I remember you getting a letter," she said in a quiet voice.

"Yeah. Then you laughed at how I said *grandmomma*." Autumn deliberately didn't hide her accent, daring Bree to imitate it again.

"It's like you think I'm not as good as you because I'm from the country. Or maybe because your family has more money than mine," Autumn continued.

Bree started to argue, then stopped. "Maybe at first," she admitted quietly. "A little. I mean, maybe I thought you'd act like people from the sticks always do on television."

Autumn rolled her eyes. "Those are *stereotypes*," she said. "Don't tell me you think TV is super accurate about showing kids who use wheelchairs too?"

Bree blinked. Then she laughed. "Fair point," she said. "I hate wheelchair stereotypes."

"Me too. And rural ones," Autumn said.

Bree stopped laughing. "I'm sorry," she said. "That wasn't cool."

Autumn took a deep breath. "Thanks. And sorry I've been a little intense on the court."

"A little?" Bree said, only half-joking.

"Okay, a lot," Autumn admitted. "Guess I feel like I have a lot to prove—and not much time to do it."

"You're a great player," Bree said. "It's hard to believe you've never played on a team."

"I would if we had one close enough," Autumn said.

Bree's eyes widened. "Just how far out do you live?"

"Far enough that there isn't reliable internet at our house," Autumn said.

Bree didn't laugh. "Wow," she said. "But it's nice that your grandma sends you letters and stuff," she added thoughtfully. "I wish my parents did that."

Autumn suddenly wondered who Bree was upset with on the phone a few days ago. "Do you get along with your parents?" she asked.

Bree shrugged. "Sometimes. When I can be perfect enough for them."

Autumn remembered what Keoko had said back in the break room. *Everyone's carrying some sort of load—no matter how shiny things look on the outside.*

\* \* \*

Autumn felt better after talking to Bree. More sure of herself, more confident that she belonged here.

And that helped her find the courage to fix something she knew needed it. She thought about it all that evening and the next day. Finally, she knew what she had to do. After thinking about it even more, she got up the courage to ask her roommates to help her.

The evening before the final game, Autumn called an emergency meeting of the staff appreciation committee. She also brought along three last-minute new members—Ashti, Coral, and Bree.

"What's this about, Autumn?" Junta asked when they'd all assembled. She looked in confusion at Autumn's roommates.

"This meeting is about speaking up for what's right," Autumn said. She took a deep breath and reminded herself she had as much right to voice her opinions as anyone else here. "At first, I didn't think I belonged here because . . . well, for a lot of reasons. But then I realized I'd definitely never fit in if I didn't believe I could. It took me a while, but I believe it now."

The other girls looked confused but listened.

Autumn continued. "I called this meeting because it's not right for us to thank some staff members and not others. So, I think we need to re-vote on that. And then fix it."

Junta spoke up. "Okay, maybe I see your point. But we've used up the money we had for gifts. And it's too late to get anything else."

Ashti piped up. "No problem. My parents live right in town. They said they'd be happy to pick up anything we wanted. They can do it tonight."

Coral chimed in too. "Since we're the late arrivals, Ashti, Bree, and I are going to chip in for the gift for the facilities staff."

"Facilities?" Junta echoed.

"Dining, housekeeping, and maintenance," Autumn explained.

"What should we get them?" Consuela asked.

Autumn grinned, remembering the tin of cookies and other snacks in the facilities break room. "I know just the thing."

They took a vote. It was almost unanimous.

Autumn didn't have much time to enjoy her victory. The big game was tomorrow, and the girls were pushing hard to get ready. Autumn could barely sleep that night, excited about seeing Marmee but sad that camp was ending. So much had changed in just two short weeks.

"You feel nervous?" Ashti asked sleepily from the next bed.

"A little," Autumn told her. "But mostly just happy."

# CHAPTER 10

# GAME NIGHT!

Two weeks had passed in the blink of an eye. Already, game night had arrived.

Autumn's nerves jangled as she took her place in the lineup. There were twenty girls playing in two exhibition games. She and Bree both ended up on Tara's team.

As she rolled onto the court with her teammates, Autumn felt a surge of pride and excitement. For the first time since camp had started, the bleachers were full of people. Parents, grandparents, even some college students and community members were there. And Marmee was there too, sitting right at half-court.

Having a real audience there—especially Marmee—made Autumn even more determined to play her best.

Autumn took her place, playing point guard opposite Laquiana, and took a deep breath.

Laquiana grinned in a teasing way. "You got what it takes, Holloway?"

Autumn grinned back. "You better believe it!"

The two forwards squared off in the center circle. The ref tossed the ball.

The game was on!

The first half was fast-paced and physical. Laquiana made Autumn fight for all she was worth. The girls competed, flying all over the court, protecting their basket and attacking opponents, stealing the ball and trying not to have it stolen right back.

When the halftime buzzer sounded, Autumn's team was up by two points—and she had scored the basket that put them ahead. Bree, who hadn't scored any points, kept glancing nervously at the bleachers where her parents were watching.

The second half was tighter. The other team made a basket in the third quarter, tying the score. Then Ashti sank a shot after an unexpected rebound, putting Autumn's team back into the lead.

Autumn's arms and shoulders burned from racing around the court, trying to block Laquiana, then trying to get past her. Ashti passed the ball to Autumn, who snagged it from the air and took off up the court toward the basket, dribbling furiously. Laquiana grabbed for the ball, and Autumn scooped it into her lap to keep it safe.

The ref's whistle shrilled. "Number four, traveling violation!"

Autumn groaned. She'd kept the ball in her lap one push too long. The other team got possession and made it to their basket. Consuela took the shot, but it bounced off the rim.

Autumn felt a rush of relief. They were still ahead by two!

Tara called a time-out, and the girls huddled up at the sidelines.

"Okay," Tara said. "Less than two minutes on the clock. Things are going our way, but we can't lose focus. Eyes on the ball, keep moving. Laquiana's defense is hot tonight, so watch out for her. And don't forget to pass if you get into a jam! That clock runs out quick. Sometimes it's better to get rid of the ball, and let someone else take the shot."

The girls all nodded and put their hands into the circle.

"Let's do this!" Tara shouted.

"One, two, three . . . TEAMWORK!" the girls shouted back.

Soon they were back in play. Amira passed to Ashti, who rolled up the court like a hurricane until two defensive players' wheelchairs blocked her path. Ashti stopped, looked around, and hurled the ball to Autumn.

Autumn snagged it from the air and shoved hard on her rims, heading toward the hoop. Laquiana whirled by and snatched the ball from Autumn mid-dribble, sending them all spinning back the other way. Laquiana passed to Coral, who made the basket.

Autumn's team groaned. They were tied with just twenty seconds on the clock!

Back on offense, Autumn took the ball down the court. She weaved and spun. Her wheels and Laquiana's almost crashed, but Autumn whirled skillfully away at the last second.

Autumn's heart pounded double-time to the beat of the bouncing ball. She saw an opening up ahead. She was almost close enough to take the shot!

"Autumn! I'm open!" It was Bree. She'd made her way to the basket, her green wheelchair perfectly positioned beneath it. Her hands were raised and ready.

Autumn hesitated, glancing between her own path to the basket and Bree waiting beneath it. She really wanted to make that last basket and make Marmee proud. But Marmee would be proud of her no matter what. Autumn had already made a basket. Bree hadn't.

Autumn made a split-second choice. She spun her chair to avoid crashing into Laquiana and passed to Bree.

The ball left Bree's hands in a blurred, orange arc.

*Swish!*

*BZZZZZZ!*

Autumn's team erupted in cheers. They'd won! Autumn raced over to Bree to be the first one to give her a hug.

\* \* \*

After the game, Autumn introduced Marmee to her friends and took her on a short tour of the campus. Then it was time to get ready for the banquet.

The dining hall had been transformed. There were real tablecloths and silverware, fairy lights, and motivational basketball posters on the walls. It was like a basketball wonderland.

The dining staff were dressed in black pants and white shirts. Keoko smiled at Autumn as she came by with a tray of fancy snacks, then stayed long enough for Autumn to introduce Marmee.

The evening was a happy blur. Autumn, her friends, and their families enjoyed the delicious dinner of soup, chicken or fish, and a huge assortment of amazing desserts.

As they dug into their chocolate lava cake, Bree leaned over to Autumn. "Okay," she whispered, "maybe I underestimated the dining hall. This is really good."

Finally, it was time to present the awards. Each girl was recognized for something. When Autumn's turn came, Carlos smiled as he read the award: "Teamwork Tough."

Last up were the staff appreciation gifts. Autumn grinned as she and Consuela presented their gifts to the facilities team. Nathaniel and Keoko accepted the four dozen donuts and handmade card on everyone's behalf.

"Thanks again for paying for those," Autumn whispered to her roommates when she got back to the table.

"Thanks for the wheelchair repair lesson you gave us all," Ashti whispered back. "More than an even trade, if you ask me!"

Full of pride, Autumn looked around the table at her new friends. *I'll find a way to get back here next summer*, she promised herself.

* * *

After the banquet, Autumn introduced Marmee to a couple other dining hall staff. Marmee's eyes lit up when she saw Nathaniel. "Aren't you Benjamin Taylor's youngest?" she asked.

Nathaniel laughed. "Sure am! I moved out here about five years ago. I'm taking a college class every semester while I work full-time."

Autumn couldn't believe it. Someone from Sandy Pines lived here?

Nathaniel continued, "I should get back to visit more than I do. My dad's having a hard time keeping up with his repair business on his own."

Marmee nodded. "He does small-engine work and general repairs, right? That sort of thing is right up Autumn's alley," she added proudly.

Autumn blushed. "I only do that at home, Marmee," she protested. "And with Uncle Gary."

But Nathaniel seemed interested. "I bet my dad would be happy to have help. I can guarantee you'd get all the practice you want. He'd pay you too."

"Thanks!" Autumn felt a rush of excitement at the thought of a summer job. She could start saving up for camp next summer. Maybe even for a sports chair of her own one day!

"Autumn?" Coral and her moms had joined them. "Can you come with us to the quad for a sec?"

Leaving Marmee to chat with the adults, Autumn followed her roommates out of the dining hall. The four girls crossed the quad together, their wheels flashing bright in the pink sunset light. They stopped under a big tree, and Ashti held up a package from her lap.

"From all of us," she said.

Autumn opened the package. It was a purple, long-sleeved Blazing Hoops hoodie.

Autumn swallowed the lump in her throat and hugged them all. "You're the best," she said, wriggling into the hoodie then and there.

"We totally have to stay in touch this fall," Coral said suddenly. "Like, every day!"

"Absolutely," Autumn said. "But let's trade snail-mail addresses for that. We don't have great Wi-Fi at my house."

Coral and Ashti looked surprised but shrugged. "Sounds like fun," Ashti said. "We'll be old-school pen pals!"

Bree laughed. "I *guess* I could manage a postcard now and then," she joked.

Autumn gave Bree a teasing smile. "I *guess* I could find time to read them," she joked back.

Autumn and her roommates lingered on the quad a while longer, watching the sun go down. Autumn closed her eyes, feeling content and snug in her new hoodie. But more than anything, savoring the feeling of being exactly where she belonged.

Monica Roe grew up in a tiny farming town and spent most of her childhood holed up in a corner of the local library, where she was once almost locked in at closing time. She could also be found performing poorly in gym class, or roaming the woods and dreaming up stories. Monica has spent many years as a pediatric physical therapy provider for remote communities in rural Alaska. She also studies public health at the University of Alaska, Anchorage. Monica and her family spend summers in rural South Carolina, where they operate a small apiary and provide community education about honeybees.

# GLOSSARY

**accessible** (ak-SESS-ih-bul)—easily used or accessed by people with varying abilities

**adaptive** (uh-DAP-tiv)—designed to assist people with varying abilities

**agility** (uh-JIH-luh-tee)—the ability to move swiftly and nimbly

**maintenance** (MAYN-ten-enss)—the repair or upkeep of equipment

**maneuver** (muh-NEW-ver)—to manage into or out of a position

**Paralympics** (PAIR-uh-LIM-piks)—a series of international contests for athletes with disabilities that are associated with the Olympic Games

**push rim** (PUSH rim)—an aluminum tube covered with a small tire glued to the rims of a wheelchair; a person uses push rims to propel a wheelchair

**rural** (RUR-uhl)—having to do with the country

**scrimmage** (SKRIM-ij)—a practice game

**stereotype** (STAIR-ee-oh-type)—an overly simple opinion of a person, group, or thing

**underestimate** (UN-der-ESS-tuh-mayt)—to place too low a value on

# DISCUSSION QUESTIONS

1. Autumn arrives at wheelchair basketball camp excited to meet new friends. However, she's not sure she fits in right away. In what ways do others make Autumn feel like an outsider? Are there ways that Autumn is making herself feel like an outsider?

2. Think about the reasons that, at first, Autumn feels more comfortable with the people who work at the camp versus the campers. Why does she feel that connection?

3. Challenged Athletes Foundation is an organization that helps people with disabilities get equipment to play sports and stay active. If you could create an organization that helped people, what would it be and how would it help others?

# WRITING PROMPTS

1. Basketball means the world to Autumn. What are some ways she describes the sport that show readers how important it is to her? Write a paragraph about your favorite sport using sensory language (sight, sound, smell, etc.) to show how you feel about it.

2. Autumn is good at fixing things. Make a list of things you're good at or skills you have. Then write a possible job or career that requires that skill next to each item. Review the list when you're looking for a job someday!

3. Imagine you are Autumn a month after camp. Write a "snail mail" letter to Coral, Bree, or Ashti. Tell them what you've been up to since camp ended.

# MORE ABOUT THE SPORT

Wheelchair basketball is an extremely athletic, fast-paced sport and is among the most popular adaptive sports in the world. Wheelchairs used for playing basketball are highly specialized, with a rugged design and a wide base of support, allowing players a high level of speed and maneuverability on the court.

The rules of wheelchair basketball are very similar to those of traditional basketball, with some differences to accommodate the use of chairs on the court. For example, a player's wheelchair is considered an extension of their body in terms of contact-based fouls or other game violations.

Each team has 24 seconds to try and make a basket before losing possession of the ball. Dribbling involves bouncing the ball and pushing one's wheelchair at the same time. If a player places the ball in their lap, they are allowed to push their wheelchair twice before they must shoot, pass, or resume dribbling.

To make the sport more inclusive for different types of abilities, players are classified based on their function within the wheelchair and their disability. The classification scale ranges from 1.0 to 4.5, in 0.5 increments. This is important because, in most leagues, the five players on the court cannot exceed 14 points. This means that it may not be the best five players on a team, but the best mix of players to formulate a strategy to utilize their combined skills.

Wheelchair basketball originated in the United States in the 1940s and began as a way to help injured veterans of World War II rehabilitate. The first U.S. wheelchair basketball teams played at Veterans Administration (VA) hospitals in Massachusetts and California.

In 1960, wheelchair basketball was one of eight adaptive sports to be included in the first Paralympic Games. In the mid-1960s, the first wheelchair basketball teams for women began, with the first U.S. women's team competing in the 1968 Olympics along with the men's team.

Today in the United States, wheelchair basketball includes club and college teams. The National Wheelchair Basketball Association (NWBA) includes more than 200 teams and has also helped to establish teams in countries all over the world.

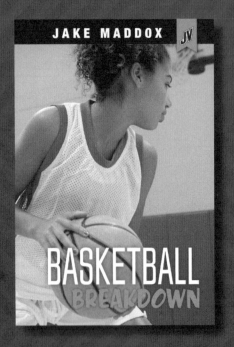